Special Smiles
THE JOURNEY OF THREE AMAZING CHILDREN

SACHIN M. SHRIDHARANI, MD & NAVIN K. SINGH, MD

Illustrations by:
Jared Travnicek
Jenny Wang

ISBN: 1451562365
ISBN-13: 9781451562361
Library of Congress Control Number: 2010905206

www.specialsmilesbook.com

Dedicated to the little princes and princess—Shyam, Simrin, and Shyer. They are the smile in my heart.

—Navin

This book is dedicated to my father who provided me with every opportunity to succeed, to my brother who has infinite insight and wisdom well beyond his years, and my mother—in her eyes, I see unconditional love.

—Sachin

PREFACE:

This book was written to commend the children who live with a cleft lip and/or palate. The courage they possess is incredible, and what they are able to overcome is amazing. These children must overcome many obstacles in their activities of daily living that many of us take for granted. Often ridiculed at school and/or shunned in their communities, these children have a level of bravery that is admirable. When we wrote this book, we had these special kids with their special smiles in mind. The journey they experience to change their appearance due to functional problems can be perilous for them and their families. We also praise the unending love that parents have for their child, which leads them to sacrifice weeks of wages, to suffer separation from their other children, and to make grueling voyages in order to help the child. We hope this book will make any child's understanding of having a cleft or knowing someone who does a more positive one.

—SMS and NKS

The authors consider themselves fortunate to be in a position to restore function to children and adults who suffer from debilitating and disfiguring problems. We have found inspiration and motivation in many places and from many people along our own special journey to become plastic surgeons. Following are just a few quotes that have stimulated our souls and incited our passion to help others.

Navin and Sachin

· · ·

"The surgeon's task is to restore, repair and make whole those parts of the face which nature has given but fortune has taken away, not so much that they might delight the eye but that they may buoy up the spirits and help the mind of the afflicted."

—Gaspare Tagliacozzi, 1546-1599
Father of modern plastic surgery

"We make a living by what we get; we make a life by what we give."
—Sir Winston Churchill, 1874-1965

"The best way to find yourself is to lose yourself in the service of others."
—Mahatma Gandhi, 1869-1948

Camp Smiles

KIM IS IN ASIA

"Papa, I had a dream last night," Kim said.

"Oh, yes my dear? And tell me, what was in that dream?" asked Kim's papa.

"I dreamed I was at a kid's camp in some place far away with other kids just like me. They all had special smiles like the one you say I have," said Kim.

"Your smile is very special. Now let's have breakfast, and then it's off to school," replied her papa.

JAMAL IS IN AFRICA

"Jamal, are you done putting that sticker on your sister's knee?" cried out Jamal's mother.

"Almost, and it isn't a sticker! It's called a Band-Aid," quickly replied Jamal.

"Okay, okay," replied his mother.

"I can't wait to be a doctor someday, Mother," later said Jamal.

"I know sweetie. You will be a wonderful doctor. You are always trying to help everyone. People feel better just from seeing your beautiful special smile. Now, we are running late for your singing class. It's time to go," said his mother.

MAYA IS IN SOUTH AMERICA

"And this is cocoa. It is where chocolate comes from," said Maya to her little brother.

"Thinking of chocolate makes me hungry," replied Pablo. "Let's go home for lunch!"

"Not yet, I want to show you this special flower," said Maya.

"I hope it is as special as your special smile," replied Pablo. "Dad always tells you and Mom how pretty your special smiles are."

"Thank you, Pablo. Nothing could be as special as you are to me though, little brother. Let's go eat!" said Maya.

Later that evening in Asia, Kim asked, "Papa, am I strange? The kids at school sometimes tease me about my strange smile."

"Not at all, my dear," replied Kim's papa. "You are not strange—just different, like my hair is different than yours, but it is not strange. Your smile is special, and you should never be ashamed."

"Sometimes though, it is hard for me to eat and drink all of the things my friends can," Kim replied back. "I want my smile to look like everyone else's, Papa."

"Of course, sweetie. If you are willing to go on a journey and promise to be brave, we will go to a place to help your smile look like everyone else's. More importantly, you will be able to eat and drink just like your friends."

"I love you, Papa. Thank you," replied Kim.

Meanwhile, after singing class in Africa, Jamal asked his mother, "How come I can't sing the same as everyone else? I try so hard, but I just can't make all of the sounds. My teacher says it is because of my special smile. Is that true?"

Jamal's mother took a leaflet out of her bag and showed it to Jamal. She said, "I love you very much, Jamal; and I think your special smile is God's gift. But, if you promise to have courage and go on an adventure with me, we can help you sing like everyone else."

Jamal replied, "Will my smile still be special after the adventure?"

"Your smile will always be God's gift to the world, Jamal," she responded.

Back in South America, Maya finished her lunch very quickly and started telling her brother about where corn kernels come from. Her dad lovingly looked at her and said, "Maya, you are going to be such a wonderful teacher one day."

"Thank you, Dad. Mom says I teach her something new every day, but I still can't figure out why I have a hard time swallowing things. Why is that?" inquired Maya.

Maya's mother responded, "Sometimes honey, something as special as your smile and my smile can also cause a problem."

"Mom, I had a dream two nights ago. In that dream, I had a new smile that looked different. It looked like everyone else's smile. But in my dream, I could swallow all drinks and food with no problems," said Maya. "Mom and Dad, I don't want to have trouble swallowing my dinner anymore."

Maya's dad said, "Maya, if you promise to be a very courageous girl, I will take you to a kid's camp where kind people will help you. Will you be brave, honey?"

Maya responded, "Yes, Dad. I will be very brave."

So, three children's journeys began. Kim and her father bicycled and walked for two days to the capital city where the special smiles kid's camp was. Big buildings surrounded them, but Kim was very brave.

Jamal and his mother took a bus and saw many animals as they navigated through the National Park. Their journey was not easy, but Jamal was not afraid.

Maya and her mother and father used their canoe and rafted down a wild river through mountain valleys. Ahead in the clearing Maya saw her special smiles kids' camp. She was nervous, but knew everything was going to be fine.

All three children were on a journey to change their special smiles so they could eat, sing, and swallow easier just like all of their friends.

When the children arrived at the kid's camp, they were surrounded by people wearing strange clothes and saying words that they did not understand. Very quickly though, they noticed other children around them with smiles as special as their own.

Much to her surprise, Kim saw Nurse Li at the camp. She remembered Nurse Li from her home town. Nurse Li gave Kim a hug and explained that twice a year she comes to this kid's camp to help little boys and girls and then teach other nurses how to take care of kids who also can't eat and drink well. Kim knew right away she belonged at this camp.

A little while later, Kim was greeted by a woman with a funny cap. She introduced herself as Doctor Angela from New York and told Kim and her papa that she was going to help Kim eat and drink like other kids. All she wanted Kim to do is be brave. Even though Kim was nervous, she knew Doctor Angela wanted to help her, and Kim agreed to be the bravest girl in the world.

Meanwhile, Jamal could not help but be excited to see so many kids who had smiles like his, but also some that were different. A very nice woman with a funny mask came up to Jamal and his mother. She said her name was Doctor Geeta from Singapore, and she was going to help Jamal sing every note in all of his favorite songs. She was an anesthesiologist and was going to make sure that he would be asleep and feel no pain during the operation. All she needed from Jamal was for him to be strong, and in a few hours his smile would still be special but look different.

Jamal quickly responded, "Not only will I be courageous, but I will also sing those notes for you!"

Dr. Geeta then explained that she had spoken to Jamal's dentist, Dr. Amar. He had called Dr. Geeta all the way from Africa because he had known Jamal since he was just a baby, and knew him better than any other doctor. They had come up with a plan and knew that they were going to be able to help Jamal.

Maya already was trying to teach an old friend about birds flying around the kid's camp. Maya saw Dr. Manny, a burn surgeon from her home town who had come to the kid's camp to help fellow doctors and nurses who had travelled from far away. He introduced Maya and her parents to Doctor Malik, a plastic surgeon from the Middle East. He wore a strange coat. He told Maya that he had come to help children just like her swallow normally. If she would agree to be bold, he would be very happy to help her.

Maya responded, "Even though I am a little afraid, I can't wait to drink my hot cocoa without problems. I will be very bold, Doctor Malik."

During the next few days, Kim, Jamal, and Maya had help from six very nice people, some old friends from their home towns and some new friends who had come from all over the world to help them.

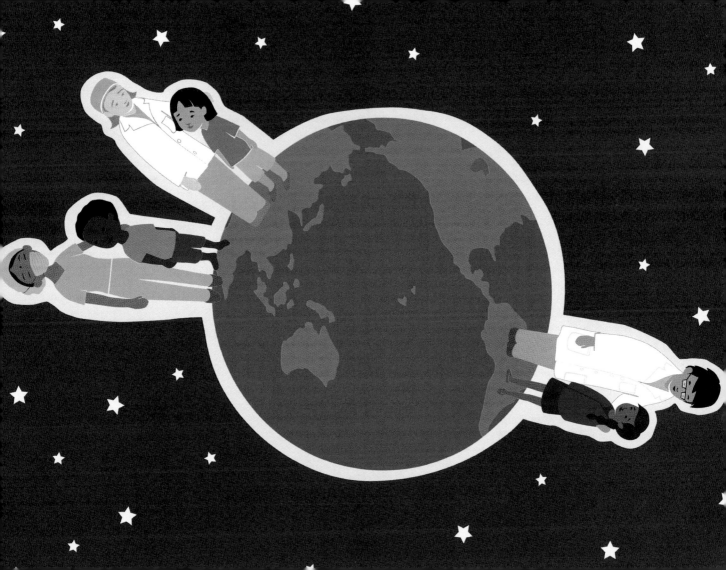

After she woke up from the operation, Kim told her daddy, "My lip feels like that time I got stung by a bee, Papa. Why is that?"

Her papa said, "My dear, in order to help you eat and drink better, Doctor Angela had to make some changes to your lip. Just like the bee sting, this feeling too, will go away."

In his hospital bed, Jamal asked his mother, "My lip feels like it has strings in it. Why is that?"

Jamal's mother responded, "Sweetie, in order to help you sing better, the doctor had to change your lip and put stitches in it to make it heal. It is like the sticker you put on your sister's knee. Don't worry; the feeling of those strings will go away in a few days."

"Mother, it's a Band-Aid, not a sticker!" Jamal replied with a little smile.

Just before taking her medicine, Maya asked her mom and dad, "My mouth feels like that time I bumped it on Pablo's head when we were playing. Why is that?"

Maya's mom replied, "Honey, in order to help you swallow better, Dr. Malik had to change the inside and outside of your mouth. Just how the feeling went away after you bumped your mouth on your brother's head, this feeling will also go away. I promise."

"When can I have chocolate?" joked Maya.

"Very soon," replied her dad.

After a few days, Kim, Jamal, and Maya were all ready to go home. They saw other children coming to their kid's camp. Kim noticed that the other children were arriving with their parents just like she had. Jamal noticed that the other children's special smiles looked like the one he used to have before he met his new role model, Doctor Geeta. He was going to study hard at school so he could become a doctor like Dr. Geeta and continue to help others. Maya noticed that new children arriving were excitedly asking their parents if they would be able to swallow ice cream like other children. She would love to become a school teacher and teach them all about the adventures that await them.

Kim, Jamal, and Maya all smiled their new smiles filled with happiness and joy as they realized they were going back home to be with friends and family. Each child told their new doctor friends goodbye.

As Kim returned to her village in Asia, she noticed that kids at school no longer teased her. Even more importantly, she ate and drank to her heart's content. She was able to share lunch at school and never had to think about if she could have noodle soup, which had become her new favorite food. She even went to visit Nurse Li a couple of times to thank her for everything. Kim and her papa were very happy.

Meanwhile, Jamal jumped for joy in his small town in Africa.
He got the lead role for a musical that was to be performed in
his school. He could now sing all of the notes. He told his mother
that he might become a professional singer one day instead of a
doctor. His mother laughed and lovingly told him he would be good
at anything he put his mind to.

Back near the Amazon River, Maya raced Pablo home after they went fishing. She was so thirsty that she drank a tumbler full of fresh lemonade. Not a single drop leaked from her mouth. She was thrilled to be able to drink just like her brother and father.

"Mom, if you promise to be brave, Dr. Malik and Dr. Manny said they would help you drink better and change your special smile next year. Will you be brave, Mom?"

"I will, Maya. Thank you, honey," replied Maya's mother.

With a little bit of bravery and courage, Kim, Jamal, and Maya were all able to eat, drink, sing, and swallow like all other children. It wasn't easy, but with loving parents and the willingness to go on an adventure and journey, these three bold children were no longer teased and were able to do all of the things they wanted to do.

22346254R00027

Made in the USA
Charleston, SC
18 September 2013